ROBOT
INVASION

Sue Graves

D1097354

sundance™

Published by Sundance Publishing
33 Boston Post Road West, Suite 440, Marlborough, MA 01752
www.sundancepub.com

First published 2009 by
Rising Stars UK Ltd., 22 Grafton Street, London W1S 4EX

ISBN: 978-1-4207-3029-6

Printed by Nordica International Ltd.
Manufactured in Guangzhou, China
September, 2016
Nordica Job #: CA21601452
Sundance/Newbridge PO #: 228538

CHAPTER 1

Kojo had just moved into a new apartment
and was really excited about his new home.
He decided to have a housewarming party on
Saturday and invited Tom and Sima to come.

Tom, Sima, and Kojo worked together at
Dangerous Games, a computer games company.
Sima came up with the ideas and designed the
games. Then Kojo programmed the games, and
Tom tested them. They were great jobs.

"The party's going to be a lot of fun," said Kojo.
"It's a sci-fi theme so you've got to come in
costume."

"Cool!" said Tom. "I love science fiction movies."

"And I know *just* what to wear," said Sima,
smiling.

On Saturday, Tom and Sima went to Kojo's party.

"Wow, Sima, you're the best-looking alien I've ever seen," said Tom. Sima blushed beneath her silver makeup.

Kojo and his friends were having a great time. Kojo's outfit was incredible. He was dressed as a robot and had even made a robot arm to hold his punch!

But Kojo's costume turned out to be a problem when he tried to speak with Ellie. She worked in the next office at Dangerous Games, and Kojo had liked her for ages. When Kojo turned to speak to Ellie, his robot arm spilled punch all over her. Ellie was embarrassed, and she was really upset with Kojo.

"You're *sooo* clumsy!" she said, as she walked off.

Kojo felt terrible.

Tom and Sima went over to Kojo.

"It looks like humans and robots don't get along," said Tom. "Maybe you need to get a robot girlfriend!"

Kojo smiled, but Sima looked thoughtful.

"Uh-oh!" said Tom, looking at Sima. "When she gets quiet like that, she's planning something."

Sima laughed. "I was thinking about what you said."

"About Kojo getting a robot girlfriend?" said Tom.

"No, not that. It was when you said that humans and robots don't get along," said Sima.

"You've lost me!" said Kojo, looking puzzled.

"It's given me an idea for a new computer game," said Sima. "I'll tell you about it on Monday at work, but for now, let's party!"

CHAPTER 2

Sima was already hard at work when Tom and Kojo got to the office on Monday morning.

"So what's your idea for a new computer game?" asked Tom, as he peered over her shoulder.

"I'm designing a game with robots in it," said Sima. "I thought the humans could try to outwit the robots."

"Nice one, Sima," said Kojo. "I'm glad my robot outfit helped you think of an idea because it sure didn't help me get a girlfriend!" He made a face.

"I know what will cheer you up, Kojo," said Tom. "Let's have some fun with this game and test it for real like we've done before."

"You're on!" said Kojo and Sima.

Sima worked on the designs all day. Then she gave them to Kojo for him to program. The game was really complicated.

On Friday, Kojo was still working hard on the game.

"This program is a nightmare!" said Kojo. He looked worried.

"What's up?" asked Tom.

"There's a problem with the number instruction, and I can't program how many robots are in the game," said Kojo.

"Is that important?" asked Sima.

"I don't know," Kojo replied. "It could cause problems."

"Don't worry about it," said Tom. "Let's test the game tonight after work, and then we'll see if it's OK or not."

Tom, Sima, and Kojo waited for everyone to leave the office. Fred, the janitor, took forever to empty all the trash cans.

"I wish he'd hurry up," Sima said to Kojo. "The stores are open late tonight, and I promised my mom I'd go shopping with her. She wants me to help her find a dress. She'll kill me if I'm late."

Finally Fred finished, and the office was empty at last.

Kojo started up the game.

"OK," he said. "Don't forget, we all have to touch the screen at the same time to enter the game, and it's only over when we hear the words *Game over.*"

"Got it," said Tom and Sima.

They all touched the screen and shut their eyes tightly as a bright light flashed.

CHAPTER 3

The bright light faded, and they opened their eyes. They were standing in the control room of a huge spaceship traveling through space. Along one wall was the biggest computer they had ever seen.

"This is awesome, Sima," said Tom. "I didn't know we'd get to travel in a spaceship. I've always wanted to do this."

"I know," said Sima beaming, "I thought I'd surprise you." Suddenly, a door at the end of the room slid open.

Standing in the doorway was a large robot made of gray metal. It had three long, bending arms, each with a metal claw at the end. Its head was an oval computer, and its eyes were lights that flashed red. The robot floated on a cushion of air as it moved slowly toward them.

"I am Titan, the master of all robots!" it said. "I have been expecting you."

"Cool," said Tom. "Where's the party? I could go for a sandwich!"

Sima and Kojo laughed, but Titan's eyes flashed more brightly.

CAN WE GET ON WITH THE GAME? I'VE GOT A LOT TO DO TONIGHT.

Tom carefully looked Titan over, tapping on the robot's metal body.

"We have to outwit the robots, right Sima?" he said. "Well, let's get on with it. It's not going to take long to outwit a heap of scrap metal like this!"

"Be careful, Tom!" said Kojo nervously.

But it was too late. Titan's eyes began to flash angrily. He made a roaring noise and pushed Tom against the wall of the spaceship. One of his claws grabbed Tom and lifted him up into the air.

Just then another door slid open,
and three more robots marched into
the room.

TAKE
THESE
HUMANS
TO THE
HOLD.

The robots grabbed Sima, Tom, and Kojo and
took them down into the hold of the spaceship.
Titan followed them.

In the hold, they saw thousands of motionless
robots standing in long lines.

"This is my army," said Titan proudly.

Kojo sighed. "I knew I should have worked out the problem with the number instruction when I was programming the game," he whispered to Tom. "How can we outwit all of these robots?"

"They're not activated," replied Tom. "It'll be fine. Don't worry!"

"In 45 minutes we land on Earth, and the invasion will begin," said Titan. "When I key the password into the computer, the robots will be activated. Then they will rule the human race!"

CAN I WORRY NOW?

Titan pushed a button on the wall, and a door slid open. Beyond it was a small, bare cell. The robots pushed Sima, Tom, and Kojo inside.

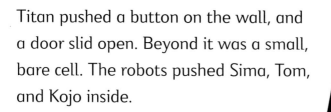

YOU WILL STAY HERE UNTIL THE INVASION IS OVER. I WILL DEAL WITH YOU LAST OF ALL. AND BECAUSE OF YOUR RUDENESS, I WILL MAKE SURE YOUR PUNISHMENT IS SEVERE!

Titan pressed another button, and the door closed behind them. There was no way out.

CHAPTER 4

Sima sat on the floor with her head in her hands.

"What are we going to do now?" she said. "My stupid game has put the whole world in danger of an attack. I wish I'd never thought of it."

Tom sat down beside her and tried to make her feel better.

HEY, IT'S NOT YOUR FAULT. WHO KNOWS, THIS INVASION MAY HAVE HAPPENED ANYWAY.

They sat in silence for a while, and then Kojo spoke.

"The game was for humans to outwit robots, right?" he said.

"Yes," said Sima, "but how can we do that when we're locked up in a cell?"

"We've got to find a way out and fast," said Tom.

Kojo pointed to the CCTV camera. "See that security camera?" he said.

I THINK I'VE GOT A PLAN.

Kojo pulled out his cell phone.

"My brother and I were extras in a war movie last year," he explained. "We played soldiers in a battle scene, and I just happen to have a video clip of the scene on my phone."

"How's that going to help?" asked Tom.

"Come here, and I'll show you," said Kojo.

Kojo climbed up on Tom's shoulders and held his phone in front of the security camera. He played the video clip of soldiers fighting in a battle.

"I programmed the game, remember. I know that the robots are only programmed to see what's in front of them," said Kojo. "They can't tell what's happening behind them."

"Go on," said Tom.

"If we stand on either side of the door when they come in," said Kojo, "we can grab them from behind and disable them. Go for the yellow wires at the back of the neck."

"Good plan!" said Tom.

Soon they heard the robots moving outside the cell. Kojo jumped off Tom's shoulders, and they pressed themselves against the wall on each side of the door.

Three robots came into the room.

Sima, Tom, and Kojo grabbed them from behind and tugged at the yellow wires, disabling them.

"Look, these robots have hollow bodies," said Tom. He tapped one of the robots. "We can hide inside them, and Titan won't know it's us."

"Cool!" said Sima. "But how are we going to stop the invasion?"

Kojo thought for a minute and then grinned. "Get inside the robots," he said. "Then follow me!"

CHAPTER 5

Tom, Sima, and Kojo got inside the robots and figured out how to make them move. Then they left the cell and went up to the control room. Other robots were coming and going, so it was easy to sneak in.

Titan was over by the window flying the spaceship toward Earth. He didn't even notice the three newcomers. Kojo moved quietly over to the computer.

"I need to reprogram the computer so that it crashes when Titan keys in the password," he whispered.

"But we don't know the password!" said Sima.

"I've got a hunch what it might be," said Kojo.

He worked at the computer for a few minutes.

Kojo yelled in triumph. Sima kicked him, but it was too late. Titan had already turned around. He saw what Kojo was doing.

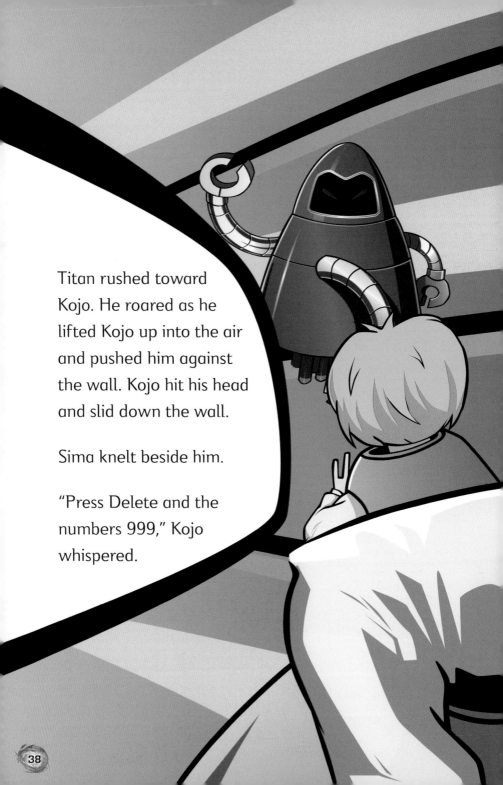

Titan rushed toward Kojo. He roared as he lifted Kojo up into the air and pushed him against the wall. Kojo hit his head and slid down the wall.

Sima knelt beside him.

"Press Delete and the numbers 999," Kojo whispered.

Sima ran toward the computer, but Titan went after her and swiped at her with his arms. She fell hard against the keyboard.

Tom pushed Titan off Sima and tried to shield her.

Quickly Sima pressed Delete and the numbers 999.

"You fools!" Titan bellowed. "You can't outwit me! No human can outwit a robot."

Titan punched in the password on the keyboard with his third arm.

"Let the invasion begin," he said, laughing horribly.

But suddenly a siren sounded. The computer flashed and sparked before it exploded into a thousand pieces. Titan's grip on Sima and Tom became weaker and weaker. One by one, the robot's lights went out, and the room became quiet.

WE'VE DONE IT! WE'VE OUTWITTED TITAN!

Just then, there was a bright light. Sima, Tom, and Kojo shut their eyes tightly.

A loud voice said, "Game over!"

The light faded. When they opened their eyes, they were back in the office.

"Phew! I'm glad that's over," said Sima. "That was the scariest game ever. How did you guess the correct password, Kojo?"

"Titan was so full of himself," replied Kojo. "I was sure the password would be *Titan*, and luckily for us, it was."

Sima frowned. "Suppose you'd guessed the wrong password," she said. "What would have happened?"

Kojo shut down his computer. He looked serious.

"We wouldn't have survived," he said. Then he smiled. "And your mom would have killed you for missing your shopping trip!"

"You can't be killed twice!" said Tom.

"You don't know my mom!" said Sima, as she grabbed her bag and ran out of the door.

Glossary of Terms

activate to make a piece of equipment start working

CCTV (Closed Circuit Television) a way of guarding an area where cameras record what is happening and show it on a television screen

control room the place in a spaceship where the main computer and controls are

disable to stop a piece of equipment from working properly

extras people who have small parts in a movie, for example, as part of a crowd

hold the place in a plane or ship where goods or luggage are kept

invasion when an army goes into another country to take control of it

outwit to get an advantage over someone using a clever trick

program to write instructions for a computer to tell it what to do

sci-fi (science fiction) a type of movie or story that imagines what might be possible in the future or in other worlds

THINK ABOUT IT

1. If you were going to have a party with a theme, what theme would you choose? Why?

2. What happens at the party to give Sima an idea for a new computer game?

3. Why does Kojo tell Tom to be careful when he speaks rudely to Titan?

4. Why is it important for Kojo to reprogram the spaceship's computer before Titan keys in his password?

5. Why must Sima hit Delete and enter the numbers 999 before Titan keys in his password?

About the Author

Sue Graves has taught school for thirty years. She has been writing for more than ten years and has written well over a hundred books for children and young adults.

"Nearly everyone loves computer games. They are popular with all age groups—especially young adults. But I've often thought it would be amazing to play a computer game for real. To be in on the action would be the best experience ever! That's why I wrote these stories. I hope you enjoy reading them as much as I've enjoyed writing them for you."

READ STREET WARS FIRST TO FIND OUT HOW THE ADVENTURE BEGINS!